If I'd Known Then
What I Know Now

By Reeve Lindbergh

Pictures by Kimberly Bulcken Root

PUFFIN BOOKS

PUFFIN BOOKS
Published by the Penguin Group
Penguin Books USA Inc., 375 Hudson Street, New York, New York 10014, U.S.A.
Penguin Books Ltd, 27 Wrights Lane, London W8 5TZ, England
Penguin Books Australia Ltd, Ringwood, Victoria, Australia
Penguin Books Canada Ltd, 10 Alcorn Avenue, Toronto, Ontario, Canada M4V 3B2
Penguin Books (N.Z.) Ltd, 182–190 Wairau Road, Auckland 10, New Zealand

Penguin Books Ltd, Registered Offices: Harmondsworth, Middlesex, England

First published in the United States of America by Viking, a division of Penguin Books USA Inc., 1994
Published in Puffin Books, 1996

1 3 5 7 9 10 8 6 4 2

THE LIBRARY OF CONGRESS HAS CATALOGED THE VIKING EDITION AS FOLLOWS:
Lindbergh, Reeve.
If I'd known then what I know now / by Reeve Lindbergh;
pictures by Kimberly Bulcken Root. p. cm.
Summary: A father's love for his family is expressed through his well-meaning but
unsuccessful attempts to fix up their house.
ISBN 0-670-85351-8
[1. Dwellings—Fiction. 2. Fathers—Fiction. 3. Stories in rhyme.]
I. Root, Kimberly Bulcken, ill. II. Title.
PZ8.3.L6148If   1994   [E]—dc20
93–24058   CIP   AC

Puffin Books ISBN 0-14-055772-5

Printed in the U.S.A.

To Amelia — with love

— R. L.

For Jake, Sue, Chrissy,

Bethany and Zack

— K. B. R.

We built this house when I was one
(My dad was just learning how).
Through the holes in the roof you can see the sun
And when it rains we have buckets of fun.
My dad says, "Son, it would be all done
If I'd known then what I know now!"

We put in plumbing when I was two
(My dad was just learning how).
When my mom takes a bath and lets it drain

The soap bubbles go right down the lane.
Dad says, "The neighbors would never complain
If I'd known then what I know now!"

We did the wiring when I was three
(My dad was just learning how).

When we flipped the switch by the new TV

The cat lit up like a Christmas tree.
Dad says, "That cat wouldn't hiss at me
If I'd known then what I know now!"

We made the cradle when I was four
(My dad was just learning how).
The baby rocked all through the night

(She could rock to the left, but not to the right).

Dad says, "Those rockers would stay on tight
If I'd known then what I know now!"

We built the kitchen when I was five
(My dad was just learning how).
The stove gets cold and the fridge gets warm
And the sink fell down in a thunderstorm.
Dad says, "They'd all be in perfect form
If I'd known then what I know now!"

We put up the chimney when I was six
(My dad was just learning how).

The smoke stays in and the fire goes out
And the wind blows the cinders all about.
Dad says, "You'd love this, without a doubt
If I'd known then what I know now!"

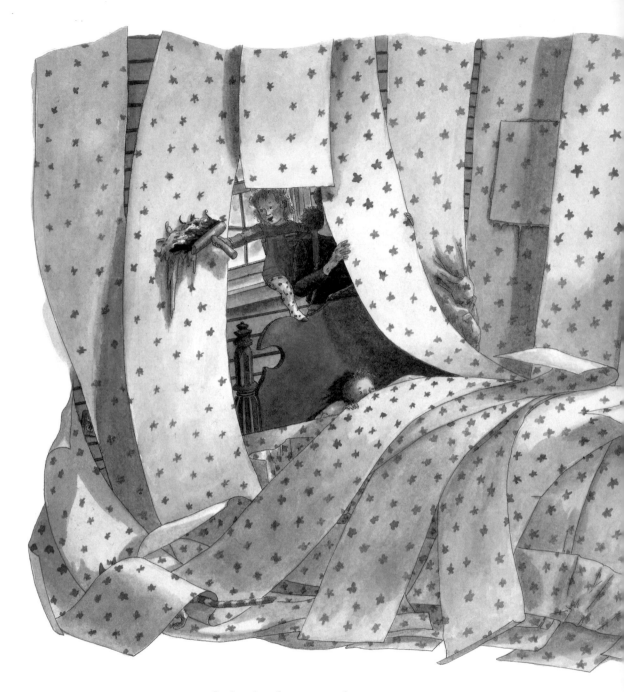

We papered the bedroom when I was seven
(My dad was just learning how).
We papered the windows, we papered the door,

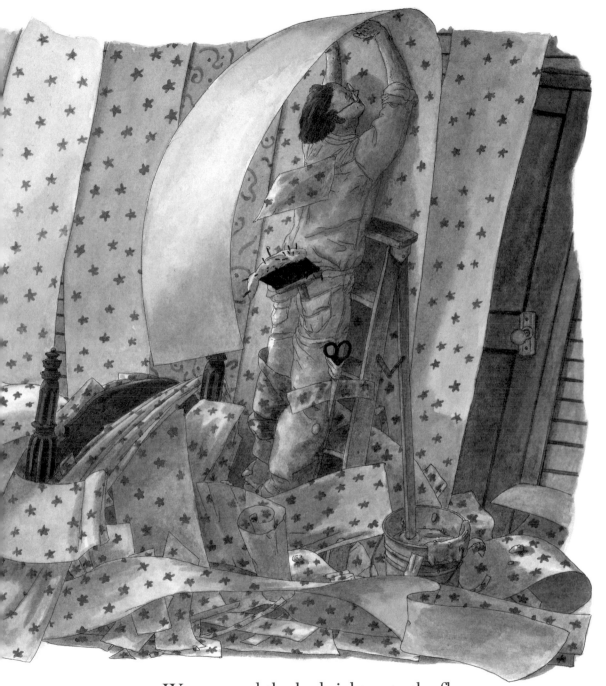

We papered the bed right onto the floor.
Dad says, "A nap wouldn't be a chore
If I'd known then what I know now!"

We made chairs and a table when I was eight
(My dad was just learning how).
The chairs are too short and the table's too tall,
At mealtimes you can't see my sister at all.
Dad says, "She wouldn't throw food at the wall
If I'd known then what I know now!"

We built the barn when I was nine

(My dad was just learning how).

The hay is downstairs, all sweet and soft,
And the cows climb a ladder to sleep in the loft.
Dad says, "They wouldn't keep falling off
If I'd known then what I know now!"

We got some chickens when I was ten
(My dad was just learning how).

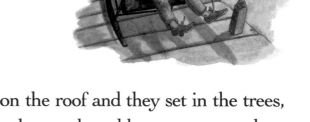

They roost on the roof and they set in the trees,
They perch on the porch and lay eggs on our knees.

Dad says, "These hens wouldn't be such a tease
If I'd known then what I know now."

We bought some sheep when I was eleven
(My dad was just learning how).
The ewes chase the chickens, the ram slams the gate,
The lambs gambol into our house at eight.
Dad says, "This flock would have been first-rate
If I'd known then what I know now."

We gave a big party when I was twelve
(My dad is still learning how).
The neighbors came, and the animals too.

We all said, "Dad, what you say is true.
But we still wouldn't want any dad but you
If we'd known then what we know now!"